Dommy B has won many poetry and performance awards, including winning New York's famous Nuyorican Poetry Café Slam, UK's Superheroes of Slam, and *Sabotage Review*'s award for Best Spoken Word Performer (twice!). He has been Glastonbury Festival's poet-in-residence and also appeared on BBC's *Rhyme Rocket*.

In 2016, Dommy B wrote *Aaaaaaaaaaaaagh! Dinosaurs!* and performed it at the Edinburgh Fringe Festival, where it became one of *Fest*'s Top Eight Shows recommended for family audiences.

By Dommy B:

The Story of
Spark, the Goblin Wizard

The Story of
When Trolls Try to Eat Your Goldfish

The Story of
The Dragon Who Hates Poetry

The Story of—
Aaaaaaaaaaaaagh! Dinosaurs!

Dommy B's Best Adventure Ever!

THE STORY OF — AAAAAAAAAAAAAGH! DINOSAURS!

DOMMY B

Flapjack Press
flapjackpress.co.uk

Exploring the synergy between performance and the page

First published in 2016 by Flapjack Press
Salford, Gtr Manchester
flapjackpress.co.uk

Reprinted in 2018, 2021

ISBN 978-0-9932370-6-5

Cover, illustrations, author photo and Puzzles by Brink
paulneads.co.uk

Printed by Imprint Digital
Exeter, Devon
digital.imprint.co.uk

Developed in association with

Stanley Grove
Primary Academy
BRIGHT FUTURES EDUCATIONAL TRUST

Dedicated to Dave Buckley,
for being a brilliant teacher of tae kwon-do
and a friend with a heart bigger than a T-Rex.

VOLCANO ISLAND
BEWARE!
CROCODILES!
SWAMP
PORT SNOOD
CRYSTAL CLIFFS
STANDING STONES
BLAST THE DRAGON'S CAVE
DIAMOND MOUNTAINS
RIVER SOX
APPLEWOOD
RIVER TIDY
PORT ALOO
SPROUT TOWN
TOFFEE LAKE
RIVER WIGGLES
TROLL MOUNTAINS
BURDLES
OLD JAM MINES
HIGH CLIFFS
THE HIGH PEAKS
THE OLD FOREST
KANGAROO PLAINS
THE VILLAGE
BLAZE THE DRAGON'S CAVE
SAUSAGE ISLAND
FARMLAND
WASPS
GOBLIN WOODS
SHALLOW STREAM
NARROW BEACH
SEASIDE TOWN
THE GALLOPING FIELDS
FRECKLES
RED ROCK ISLAND
LOW CLIFFS

CONTENTS

CHAPTER ONE

SCARLET MEETS A DINOSAUR

Out of all the children in this small, seaside town, Scarlet is the only troll.

No other children here can play football with a boulder like Scarlet does.

No other children here can swim in the lava of a volcano like Scarlet does.

No other children here go to the seaside library every day to borrow a book like Scarlet does.

Today, Scarlet is walking down from the town to the beach, hugging her favourite library book tight, when she sees a very strange sight…

There is some sort of animal hopping about by the side of the sea.

It has a small head, a thick body and a long tail which ends in a bony club.

It looks just like a…

...dinosaur!

"Am I the only ankylosaurus on this beach? I think I am the only ankylosaurus on this beach."

The dinosaur points to the ground.

"I spent an hour talking to this guy because I thought he was an ankylosaurus too, but he's not, he's a rock.

My name's Aadya. Are those people in the picture on your book doing tae kwon-do?"

"Yes," grins Scarlet. "I love tae kwon-do!"

There are many pictures in Scarlet's library book of people practising tae kwon-do. They are jumping great heights and performing powerful kicks.

A lot of the book is about showing respect.

Scarlet has never met anyone else interested in tae kwon-do before.

"I love tae kwon-do too!" beams Aadya. "Would you like to practise with me now?"

Together, Scarlet and Aadya race into the shallow sea water.

They jump, kick, duck and dive.

Aadya can jump even higher, kick even more powerfully and duck and dive much faster than Scarlet.

Scarlet is impressed, but also just a little bit jealous.

When they finally stop to rest Scarlet says to Aadya, "I thought dinosaurs were extinct."

"Rude!" laughs Aadya. "I don't think I'm extinct. I don't remember anything before today. I don't remember how I learned tae kwon-do. I think you are the first person I've ever met."

"Oh, I am not a person," says Scarlet. "I am a troll."

"Do all trolls do tae kwon-do?" asks Aadya.

"I don't know. The only other troll I know is my Mum, and she hates everything... except carrots."

Scarlet sighs.

"Carrots are my Mum's favourite food. She eats so many carrots, all her poo is orange. Her poo is such bright orange, it glows in the dark. Yesterday, my Mum ate a hundred carrots in one go. The glow from her poo was so bright it was like the beam of a lighthouse.

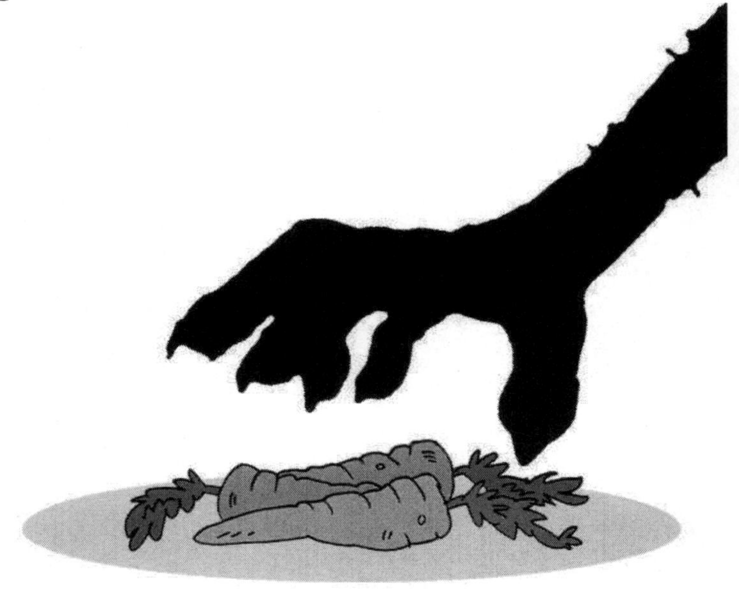

All last night, Mum kept me awake screaming for more carrots. This morning she was too sleepy to go out so I said I would get them, but then I met you. I don't want to go now."

"Don't go!" says Aadya. "Stay here. Do more tae kwon-do with me."

"No. I have to get Mum's carrots. I promised."

Scarlet waves goodbye and heads towards the town.

What Scarlet doesn't know is that today will be the last day she ever sees these shops and houses.

After what happens today, this place will never be the same again.

CHAPTER TWO

FIRST ATTACK OF THE DINOSAURS

When mighty, roaring dinosaurs
destroy the town with stomping claws
they shatter windows, roofs and floors
and make a gruesome noise.
They crush the buildings' walls and doors
as if they were just toys!

When Scarlet sees them, her jaw drops.
A terrible triceratops
is tearing up their homes and shops.
The people scream in fear,
"What if this monster never stops?"
"Why has this thing come here?"

From out the rubble leaps a raptor,
grabbing Scarlet's arm! It's trapped her!
Could this be her final chapter?
How can she get free?
Scarlet firmly asks her captor,
"Please, let go of me,"

and then she quickly twists her wrist
to free her hand and form a fist.
The raptor lunges! It has missed
for Scarlet's wise and quick.
She loudly shouts, "OK. Stop this!"
and then lets loose a kick.

The raptor's hit. It backs off, dazed.
The great triceratops is crazed.
It charges with its horns all raised
but Scarlet sees it come.
She vaults aside. She isn't fazed.
She kicks it up the bum!

Two dinosaurs have lost their fight
but one remains. It stands upright.
A T-Rex roars! Its teeth are white.
Its breath smells like cow dung.
It bows its head to try to bite
so Scarlet smacks its tongue!

Her blow connects with such a ***WHACK***
the T-Rex howls at her attack,
then all the dinosaurs step back,
turn round and run away.
They race across the cracked tarmac
for Scarlet's saved the day!

Hooray! Hooray!
Hooray! Hooray!
Because Scarlet's saved the day!
Hooray! Hooray!
Hooray! Hooray!
Because Scarlet's saved the day!

CHAPTER THREE

TEARS LIKE BOWLING BALLS

"Thank you," Scarlet blushes as the people cheer, "but I have to go now. If I don't get Mum's carrots, she will be so angry. I promise I will come back and help you mend everything after I have got Mum's carrots."

Suddenly, louder than the people cheering, Scarlet hears another noise.

BOO- HOO- HOO- HOO- HOO...

Leaving the people, Scarlet searches the wreckage of the town.

She passes the demolished diner, the mangled market and the shattered school to find the source of the sound.

BOO- HOO- HOO- HOO- HOO- HOO...

Sat in the rubble of a ruined café, is a gigantic monster with enormous red wings.

As Scarlet steps warily forward, he covers his face and growls.

**"THAT'S NOT CRYING YOU CAN HEAR.
DRAGONS NEVER CRY IN FEAR."**

"Dragon? I've never met a dragon before. I'm Scarlet. What's your name?"

**"MY NAME... IS BLAZE. THOSE DINOSAURS
ATTACKED ME WITH THEIR TEETH AND CLAWS.**

**I'D NORMALLY FIGHT BACK WITH FLAME
BUT EVER SINCE THE SUMMER CAME,
MY FIRE'S STOPPED! CAN YOU BELIEVE A
DRAGON LIKE ME HAS... HAY FEVER?!**

ALL BUNGED UP, MY FLAMES WON'T HURL.
THEY SAID THAT I FIGHT LIKE A *GIRL*!

I'M NOT A GIRL. THAT ISN'T TRUE.
AH-AH... AH-AH... AH-AHHHHHHH... AH-CHOO!!"

From Blaze's bunged up nose he sneezes a hot stream of sticky snot.

"I am sorry those dinosaurs were mean to you, Blaze," says Scarlet. "I don't think a boy being like a girl is a bad thing. I met a girl called Aadya this morning who is the best fighter I have ever seen.

I am going to find Aadya and ask her if she'll help me find those dinosaurs and make them stop. I know it will make my Mum angry, but she is just going to have to wait for her carrots."

Blaze watches as Scarlet starts to stride away.

"WAIT! CAN I COME? TELL ME WHY YOU'D WANT TO WALK WHEN YOU COULD... FLY?"

Blaze spreads out his colossal wings.

"PLEASE, SCARLET. I BELIEVE IN YOU. AH-AH... AH-AH... AH-AHHHHHHH... AH-CHOO!!"

Scarlet jumps onto the snuffly dragon's back.

Together, the two new friends soar into the sky and begin their quest to find Aadya and stop the deadly dangerous dinosaurs.

CHAPTER FOUR

WHERE DID THE DINOSAURS COME FROM?

Meanwhile, far away from Scarlet and Blaze, in a grassy clearing in a big forest, there lives a goblin wizard.

This goblin's name is Spark.

Being a wizard, Spark knows how to use magic to transform anything.

If he's hungry, he can transform a tiny acorn into a massive roast dinner.

If he's thirsty, he can transform a blade of grass into a river of lemonade.

Yesterday, a very odd thing happened.

Spark had been wandering through the forest, looking for a nice spot to take the twelfth of the twenty-five naps he likes to have every day.

However, wherever he went he kept finding hot, sticky piles of snot, big as buses, all over the woods.

Spark had been bored, so he had decided to use his magic to transform the piles of snot into something else.

From this snot, he had created –

a terrifying triceratops,

a raging raptor,

a towering T-Rex,

and finally, an ankylosaurus with a passion for tae kwon-do.

Spark's plan had been to watch them fight each other until he got tired and then transform the dinosaurs into some fluffy pillows and a cosy quilt.

"If Grandma was here, she would go on and on about 'respect'. Well, Grandma's not here right now, is she? I can do anything. Ha ha! Anything! Anything!"

However, in the middle of a close match between the T-Rex and triceratops, Spark had fallen asleep.

Now that he has woken up, all of his dinosaurs have...

gone.

"Never mind," he smirks. "There are plenty more piles of snot everywhere. I will just transform this snot into something even better. I will create...

a dinosaur wizard!

A hiss of snake.
A werewolf's bark.
Transform for me.
Transform for Spark."

A burst of blue smoke puffs up into the air.

The snot transforms into the biggest dinosaur Spark has ever made.

She has a face like a grinning crocodile and a thin sail all the way down her back.

Spark has created a spinosaurus witch.

"Who are you?"

"Who am I?" Spark raises his eyebrows. "Why, I am Spark. I made you. I am going to make some more magic dinosaurs whom you will fight for my entertainment."

The spinosaurus witch slowly shakes her head.

"No. I am Fire. I am your destroyer! It is *you* I will fight for *my* entertainment! I will crush your bones into dust!

A hiss of snake.
A deep fat fryer.
Transform for me.
Transform for Fire!"

CHAPTER FIVE

MAKE IT TOUGH

"Make it *tough*.
Make it *tough*.
Really fierce and really rough.
This is not nasty enough!
Make it *tough*.
Make it *tough*.

I want to make some misery.
I want your heart to ache.
Imagine it's your birthday and
I've eaten all your cake.
Now fill the sky with thunder,
no more sunshine, only showers!
I'll go out in your garden and
I'll trample on your flowers.

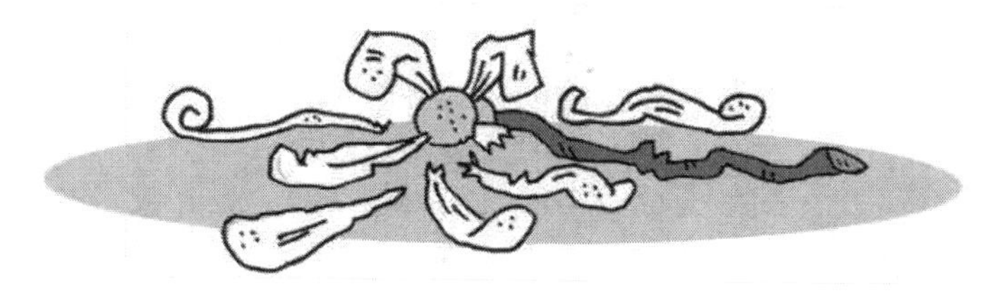

Make it *tough*.
Make it *tough*.
Really fierce and really rough.
This is not nasty enough!
Make it *tough*.
Make it *tough*

I'll make your life so nasty,
oh, as nasty as can be.
I'll make you meet a shark
if you go swimming in the sea.
I'll make you get quite badly scratched
next time you pet a cat.
I want to make it nasty
'cos nasty is where I'm at!

Make it *tough*.
Make it *tough*.
Really fierce and really rough.
Fill your world with nasty stuff.
Make it *tough*.
Make it *tough*.
Make
it
TOUGH...

A hiss of snake.
A tone deaf choir.
Transform for me.
Transform for Fire!"

CHAPTER SIX

DON'T PLAY WITH YOUR FOOD

"Please! Stop!" whimpers Spark, as Fire slings lightning bolts towards him.

"I will destroy you!"

Just in time, Spark transforms some leaves into an enormous pink mountain of jelly to block the lightning bolt attack.

Flying high in the sky, Scarlet the troll and Aadya the ankylosaurus, riding on the back of Blaze the dragon, see the commotion.

Scarlet asks Blaze to swoop down to where Spark is cowering behind his jelly wall.

"Help!" begs Spark. "I made these dinosaurs, but can't control them!"

"Oh, yeah!" gasps Aadya. "I remember! This guy made me out of a load of that snot."

"*You* made these dinosaurs?" Scarlet is furious. "A whole town was destroyed because of you!"

Blaze snuffles and snorts. With all the trees and plants around him, his hay fever is worse in the forest than it was in the town.

**"THAT WAS A FOOLISH THING TO DO.
AH-AH... AH-AH... AH-AHHHHHHH... AH-CHOO!!"**

A hot stream of snot bursts from Blaze's nostrils and splatters over Spark.

"Ugh!" gasps Spark, wiping away clumps of green goo. "Wait! This snot tastes just like the snot I used to create the dinosaurs! It *is* the same! There would be no dinosaurs if you hadn't blown your bogeys everywhere, Dragon. This is all your fault!"

At that moment, Fire's spells blow up the wall.

"Now I've got you!"

A bolt of magic from Fire's left hand transforms Spark into a burger and chips.

A bolt of magic from Fire's right hand transforms Blaze into a falafel wrap dripping with hummus.

A bolt of magic from Fire's left foot transforms Aadya into a mustard smothered hotdog.

Fire can only cast three spells at a time (she needs her right foot to stand on!).

Scarlet must move fast before Fire's next attack.

If Fire beats Scarlet, she will never get the carrots for her Mum.

If Fire beats Scarlet, she will never be able to help mend the town that the dinosaurs destroyed.

Worse than that, if Fire beats Scarlet, her new friends might stay as food forever.

Worse than that, Fire might eat them!

"You're next!"

Never has Scarlet needed tae kwon-do more than now.

CHAPTER SEVEN

FIRE!

Emergency! Will Scarlet win this fight?
She turns to see a witch's spell alight.
This burning beast's big, magic hands ignite
and fervently attack with all their might!

There's Fire! Fire in the air!
This must be Scarlet's worst nightmare.
There's Fire! Fire everywhere
but Scarlet's speed's beyond compare.

There's urgency as Scarlet's feet take flight
and perfectly she jumps an awesome height.
Determinedly, she has the witch in sight.
With certainty, her kick's like dynamite!

A kick like fire in the air!
A kick like fire. Witch, beware!
A kick like fire in the chest!
Will Scarlet prove that she's the best?

Kick like fire!
Kick like fire!
Kick like fire!

CHAPTER EIGHT

FINAL ATTACK OF THE DINOSAURS

The triceratops, raptor and T-Rex have heard the battle. They stand watching Scarlet and Fire fight.

"HOW IS SCARLET SO FAST?" roars the T-Rex. **"I WANT TO BE FAST."**

"Scarlet is fast because she does tae kwon-do," replies the mustard smothered hot dog which used to be Aadya. "Isn't she ace?"

"YES! FAST! I WANT TO BE FAST. MAKE HER TEACH ME!"

"She won't be able to teach anyone anything if Fire turns her into a bag of popcorn or a bowl full of blancmange," warns Aadya. "If you want Scarlet to teach you, you should help her stop Fire."

"YES! YES! TRICERATOPS! RAPTOR! COME!"

The three dinosaurs have the witch surrounded.

The T-Rex snaps its giant teeth.

"YOU CAN'T GET US ALL. IF YOU CAST A SPELL ON ONE OF US, THE REST OF US WILL ATTACK."

"Turn my friends back to normal!" orders Scarlet.

"YES!" roars the T-Rex. **"TRICERATOPS! RAPTOR! READY!"**

The raptor hops from foot to foot, growling menacingly...

The triceratops lowers its huge, horned head and paws at the ground, preparing to charge...

"Curses!" spits Fire.

A burst of blue smoke puffs up into the air.

Blaze, Spark and Aadya are dragon, goblin and ankylosaurus once more.

Fire is furious.

"You may have won his battle, but I'll be back. When I return, I will transform you all into barbeque sauce!"

A final burst of blue smoke puffs up into the air and Fire disappears.

The spinosaurus witch is gone.

"Thank you, Scarlet," whispers Spark, sheepishly. "I'm sorry I made all this trouble. I will transform the dinosaurs back into snot."

"Don't do that!" pleads Aadya. "I don't want to be a bogey again!"

The T-Rex roars.

"WE WANT TO BE FAST LIKE SCARLET! PLEASE."

"I don't know," replies Spark. "You destroyed a whole town..."

"PLEASE!" all the dinosaurs beg.

Spark turns to Scarlet.

"Well? Scarlet? What do you think?"

CHAPTER NINE

DINOSAURS ARE BETTER THAN BOGEYS

One month has passed.

Scarlet gets her Mum the juiciest carrots she can find.

Scarlet's Mum grabs the carrots without saying thank you and gobbles them all up without offering her daughter a single one.

In the forest, Spark shouts to Blaze, "Hey! Dragon! You will never have hay fever ever again. I have transformed every plant on the planet into candyfloss."

"Please turn them back," asks Aadya. "Plants create oxygen and without that we can't breathe!"

"Whatever," grumbles Spark.

Blaze takes a deep breath.

**"I THINK I'M CURED! I TOOK A LOOK
IN SCARLET'S GREAT TAE KWON-DO BOOK.
I READ OF DIFFERENT WAYS TO BREATHE.
I LEARNED A LOT. WOULD YOU BELIEVE...**

**I NOW CONTROL MY BREATH, SO WHEN
I BREATHE LIKE THIS, I'VE FLAMES AGAIN!"**

Blaze spits a golden sheet of flame into the air.

Spark magics up a fantastic new seaside city

and Scarlet starts her own tae kwon-do club.

Scarlet, Aadya, Blaze, Spark, all the people and all the dinosaurs learn together about how to fight with respect.

"I AM FAST! I AM FAST!" roars the T-Rex.

"You know, I could just cast a magic spell," says Spark, "and transform us all into tae kwon-do masters straight away."

"But I like learning," replies Aadya.

Blaze's voice booms with pride.

**"THERE'S NO ONE BETTER THAN THIS GIRL.
THE GREATEST FIGHTER IN THE WORLD!"**

Scarlet cheers.

"But we keep learning every day.
We learn together, that's the way,
and if a villain dare comes near
then we'll be ready. We'll be here!"

PUZZLES

WICKED WORDSEARCH ONE

Spark has hidden some words below, but he cannot remember where. Can you find them? Some of them go left to right, some of them go up and down, some of them go diagonally and some of them are spelled backwards.

B	L	A	Z	E	M	C	H	G
P	F	E	J	S	D	F	A	O
A	V	T	P	N	Y	C	A	B
N	A	E	E	H	F	Q	D	L
Q	L	L	R	C	X	K	Y	I
L	B	R	I	T	Q	Z	A	N
X	Y	A	F	I	R	E	N	J
X	I	C	D	W	I	D	B	K
U	T	S	S	P	A	R	K	L

SPARK	GOBLIN
AADYA	FIRE
SCARLET	SPELL
BLAZE	WITCH

MENACING MAZE

Scarlet has to visit the library to renew her book. Can you help her find the way? Watch out for the dinosaurs!

PUZZLES

CRAFTY CROSSWORD

Can you complete this crafty crossword? Aadya has provided some clues to help you.

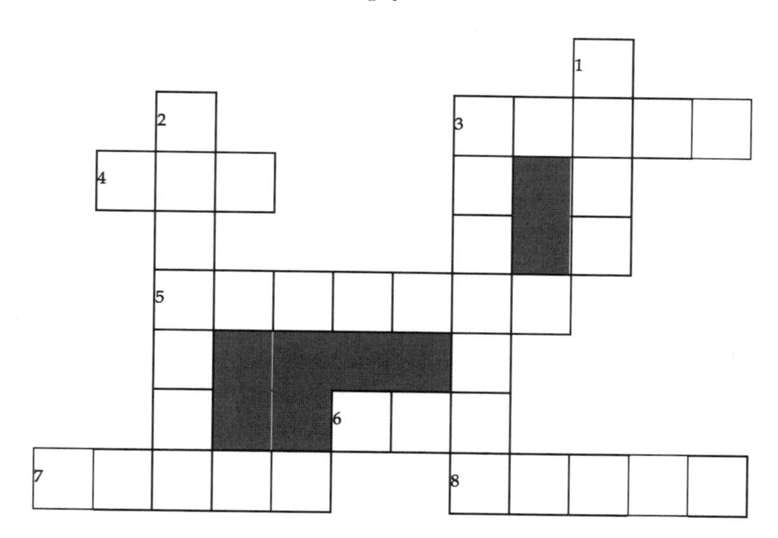

Across:

3. Dinosaurs attacked Blaze with their feet and _ _ _ _ _ (5)
4. The T-Rex's breath smells of _ _ _ dung (3)
5. Scarlet likes to borrow books from here (7)
6. Aadya is turned into a _ _ _ dog (3)
7. How many horns does a triceratops have on its head? (5)
8. Who made all the dinosaurs? (5)

Down:

1. What does the T-Rex want to be? (4)
2. Scarlet can play football with one (7)
3. Scarlet's Mum loves these! (7)

PUZZLES

WICKED WORDSEARCH TWO

Aaaaaaaaaaaaagh! Spark has done it again! He was making another wordsearch, but after a short break for lunch (when he ate four crumpets, six fairy cakes and a banana) he nodded off. Now he has woken up and cannot remember where any of the words are. Can you find them all?

T	R	I	C	E	R	A	T	O	P	S
A	K	N	N	Z	B	C	R	U	U	P
J	W	R	Z	O	S	N	O	V	J	I
R	M	O	G	K	G	N	L	K	P	N
T	A	T	Y	R	H	A	L	H	P	O
F	D	P	S	F	A	S	R	S	N	S
I	T	A	E	K	W	O	N	D	O	A
X	B	R	W	R	E	Z	E	V	U	U
C	R	R	T	R	E	X	J	D	F	R
S	R	U	A	S	O	N	I	D	W	U
P	R	F	X	N	X	K	D	Y	X	S

TROLL
DRAGON
TAEKWONDO
DINOSAURS

RAPTOR
TRICERATOPS
TREX
SPINOSAURUS

ANSWERS

WICKED WORDSEARCH ONE

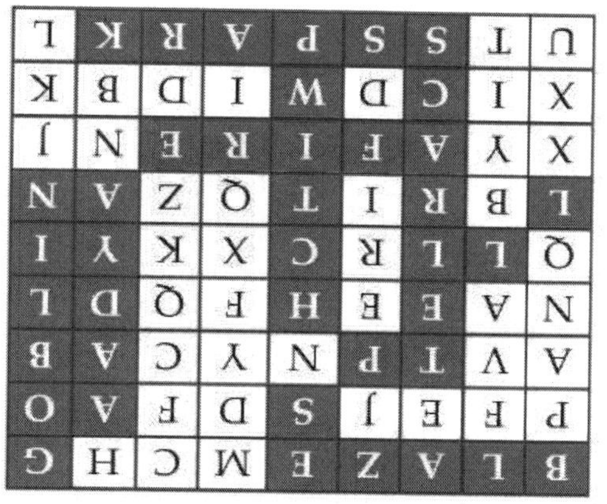

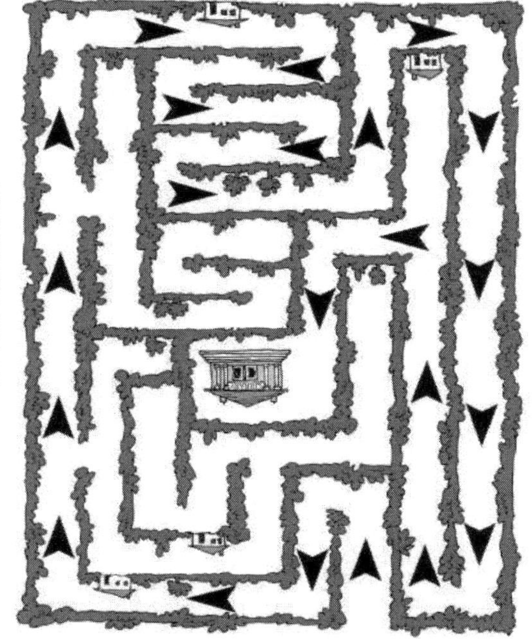

ANSWERS

CRAFTY CROSSWORD

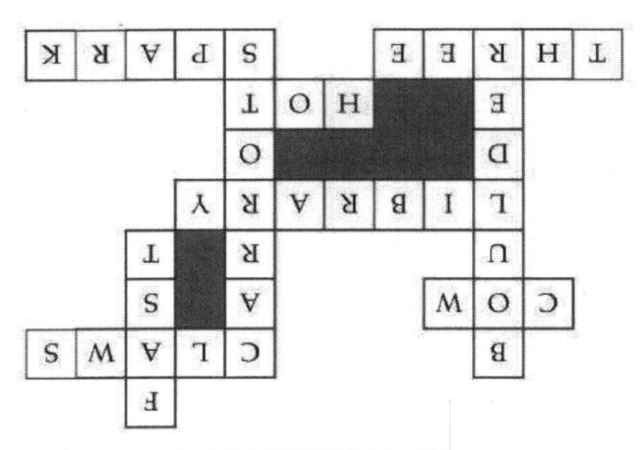

WICKED WORDSEARCH TWO

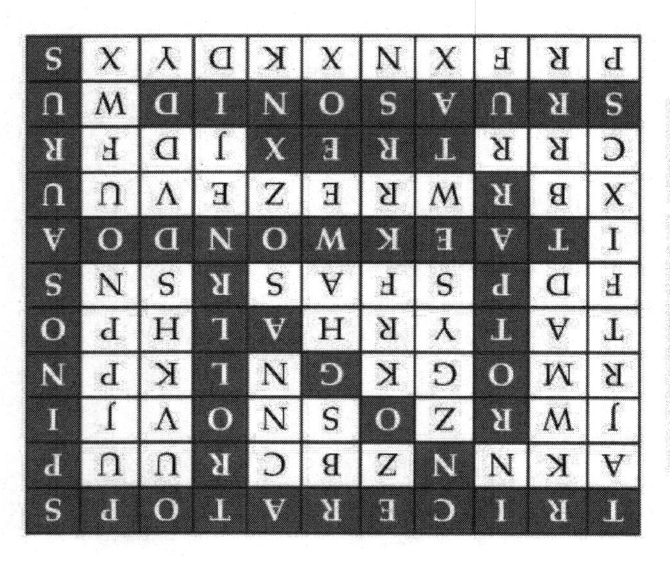